DESERTS

DESERTS

PETER MURRAY

THE CHILD'S WORLD®, INC.

PHOTO CREDITS

Comstock: 15
Dembinsky Photo Associates/Joh S. Botkin: 10
Dembinsky Photo Associates/Dominique Braud: 26
Dembinsky Photo Associates/C. Carvalho: 6
Dembinsky Photo Associates/Terry Donnelly: cover, 2, 13, 16, 19, 20, 29, 30,
Dembinsky Photo Associates/Ed Kanze: 24
Dembinsky Photo Associates/Rod Planck: 23
Tony Stone Images/Joel Bennett: 9

Library of Congress Cataloging-in-Publication Data

Murray, Peter, 1952 Sept. 29-
Deserts / Peter Murray
p.   cm.
Includes index.
Summary: Highlights a number of the world's
deserts, defines what constitutes a desert, and
describes the environment, including some of the
plants and animals that live in these arid regions.
ISBN 1-56766-280-3
1. Desert ecology—Juvenile literature.   2. Deserts—
Juvenile literature.   [1. Deserts.   2. Desert ecology.
3. Ecology.]
I. Title.
QH541.5,D4M87   1996
508.315'4—dc20   96-1571[B]
                        CIP
                        AC

TABLE OF CONTENTS

WELCOME TO THE DESERT!

In northern Africa there is a place where the sun shines every day of the year. The temperature can reach 130 degrees Fahrenheit. Sand dunes rise 1,000 feet into the air. You could walk for days and see nothing but blowing sand and buzzing flies and a few lonely patches of dry brown grass.

This is the Sahara. It is the largest desert in the world.

The Sahara desert is covered with sand

Two thousand miles away in Mongolia, there lies a land covered with gravel and boulders. Icy winds howl over this barren landscape. **Petrified** dinosaur bones are sometimes found scattered among the broken rocks. Temperatures here can drop to forty degrees below zero.

The Mongolian nomads call this place the Gobi, which means "place without water." The Gobi is a desert, too.

The Gobi desert is covered with gravel and boulders

When a place gets less than ten inches of rain per year, we call it a desert. Some deserts are hot, like the Sahara. Other deserts are cold, like the Gobi. They all have one thing in common. They are very dry. One of the driest deserts is the Atacama desert of Chile and Peru. Some parts of the Atacama have had no rainfall for hundreds of years.

The Atacama desert is the driest of all deserts

WHERE CAN YOU FIND DESERTS?

Every continent has deserts. Much of the western United States is desert. Central Australia is covered by a desert region called the outback. The southern tip of South America is largely desert. Northern Africa is covered by the Sahara, a desert as big as the mainland United States. The Arabian **peninsula**, between the Persian Gulf and the Red Sea, is almost entirely desert. A large part of central Asia, from China to the Caspian Sea, is mostly desert.

One eighth of our planet is covered by deserts.

Death Valley is a desert in the western United States

WHAT DO DESERTS LOOK LIKE?

When most people think of deserts, they think of sand. But deserts can also be covered with gravel, or a dry crust of salt, or big rocks called boulders. Some deserts, like the Atacama and the Gobi, are rocky flat areas called **plateaus**, thousands of feet above sea level. In parts of the Sahara, the sand gives way to towering mountains.

Deserts are known for their strange rock formations. The Turret Arch of Arches National Park in Utah was-formed by tens of thousands of years of blowing sand and driving rain.

Deserts have uniques rock formations, like Turret Arch in Utah

In the desert, hot days and cold nights can cause boulders to shatter. Large rocks become small rocks, small rocks turn into gravel. Gravel is broken down into sand. Gravel and sand can combine to make a hard, flat surface called desert pavement. If you didn't know better, you might think you were standing in the middle of the world's largest parking lot!

Desert pavement forms when rocks break down into sand

WHAT HAPPENS WHEN IT RAINS?

When rain does come to the desert, it doesn't stay long. The sandy, rocky desert soil will not hold water. Some rain might filter down through the sand and rock into a layer of water hundreds of feet underground. This buried layer of water is called an **aquifer**. Most of the rain, though, quickly runs off into **gullies** and streams. Sometimes the rainwater pools in large, shallow lakes called **playas**. Playas do not last long in the desert heat. The sun bakes them dry.

Rainwater creates a playa in Death Valley, New Mexico

The desert environment is too dry for most plants. Some plants, though, have adapted to this harsh **environment**. In the North American deserts, *mesquite* trees and *creosote* bushes send their roots deep into the soil. They seek out water that no other plants can reach. The *dwarf cereus* stores water in a thick, turnip-shaped root.

Short-lived flowering plants called **ephemerals** grow quickly after a rain. Within a few short weeks the ephemerals flower, drop their seeds, then die. The seeds wait for the next rainfall. Sometimes they wait for years! When the rains finally come, the seeds sprout and new plants grow.

A flower grows in the desert

In North and South America, the most familiar desert plant is the cactus. There are hundreds of types of cacti. The thick, leafless green stem of the cactus stores water like a giant sponge. Sharp spines protect the cactus from hungry animals. A waxy coating on the thick, tough skin prevents precious water from evaporating. The cactus uses water slowly. It might have to wait months for the next rainstorm.

The largest cacti—the *saguaro*—can stand more than fifty feet tall.

The saguaro cacti is the largest cacti in North and South America

WHAT ANIMALS LIVE IN THE DESERT?

Desert animals have also adapted to their dry environment. During the hot daylight hours, there is little movement. When night falls, however, the creatures come out of their hiding places. A *scorpion* crawls out from beneath a rock, hoping to find a fat beetle. Mice and rats search for seeds to eat. The snakes also come out at night. They are hunting for the mice and rats. Many of these desert creatures never need to take a drink of water. They get all the moisture they need from the food they eat.

Scorpions live in deserts

One of the largest and most famous desert creatures is the one-humped camel, or *dromedary*. Their large, webbed feet make walking on the sand easy. Their woolly coats protect them from the sun. They store fat in their humped backs. Camels can travel for many days without food or water. The **nomadic** people of the Sahara use camels to carry supplies across the desert.

In the cold Gobi desert of Asia, the nomads use another type of camel. The *Bactrian* camel has two humps instead of one. It has very thick wool to keep it warm during the cold Gobi winters.

The camel stores fat in its hump

CAN PEOPLE CREATE DESERTS?

Most of the Earth's deserts formed slowly, by natural forces. Plants, animals, and people had time to adapt to changing conditions. But today, we are seeing the growth of new deserts that are being created by people. People settle in the arid grasslands around the edges of deserts. They replace the native trees and grasses with farm crops. In very dry years, called **droughts**, the crops die. There are no trees to slow the wind. There are no native grasses to protect the soil. The soil blows away, and the sand blows in. This process is called desertification. Parts of Africa, Australia, Asia and the Americas are threatened by growing desert areas.

People can cause deserts to grow

We know we have the power to turn fertile land into desert. Can we also stop the desertification process?

People are learning how to live in and around our planet's deserts. We do not want the deserts to destroy cropland. And we do not want to ruin the natural beauty of the deserts. Deserts look like powerful, unchangeable environments, but human beings are powerful, too. Water, wind, sand, stone, sun, plants, and animals combine in special ways to create the desert ecology. If we dam up a river, trees might die. If we pollute the air, cacti might not grow. If we build a freeway, animals will not be able to cross it. Every time we change some part of the desert environment, we are playing with its delicate balance.

People are learning to protect the delicate balance of deserts

GLOSSARY

aquifer (A-kweh-fur)
A layer of water hundreds of feet underground. In deserts, some rain filters down through the sand and rocks into aquifers.

drought (DROWT)
A lack of rain, or a long period of dry weather. In drought years, crops die.

environment (en-VYE-run-ment)
Surroundings; especially, the conditions or influences that affect the development of a person, an animal, or a plant. Some species of plants have adapted to the harsh desert environment.

ephemerals (eh-FEM-er-el)
Flowering plants that live a very short time. In the desert, ephemerals grow quickly after a rain.

evaporate (e-VAP-er-ate)
Water changes into vapor or steam and disappears. Cacti have a waxy coating that keeps water from evaporating.

gully (GUL-ee)
A ditch or small ravine made by running water, often after a heavy rain. In the desert, most rainfall quickly runs off into gullies.

peninsula (peh-NIN-sull-uh)
Land that juts out into water or is almost surrounded by water. One huge desert area is the Arabian peninsula, between the Persian Gulf and the Red Sea.

petrified (PET-ri-fied)
Turn into stone, like a petrified tree. Some deserts have petrified dinosaur bones.

plateaus (pla-TOZE)
A broad, flat piece of land that is higher than the land around it. Some deserts are rocky plateaus.

playa (PLY-uh)
A large, shallow lake of rainwater. In the desert, playas sometimes form after a rain.

nomadic (no-MAD-ic)
A tribe or people who have no home, and wander from place to place. The nomadic people of the Sahara use camels to carry supplies across the desert.

INDEX